LOVE,
The Destiny to Pain...

A collection of Love poems

Spondon Ganguli

Ukiyoto Publishing

All global publishing rights are held by

Ukiyoto Publishing

Published in 2024

Content Copyright © Spondon Gaguli

ISBN

All rights reserved.
No part of this publication may be reproduced, transmitted, or stored in a retrieval system, in any form by any means, electronic, mechanical, photocopying, recording or otherwise, without the prior permission of the publisher.

The moral rights of the author have been asserted.

This is a work of fiction. Names, characters, businesses, places, events, locales, and incidents are either the products of the author's imagination or used in a fictitious manner. Any resemblance to actual persons, living or dead, or actual events is purely coincidental.

This book is sold subject to the condition that it shall not by way of trade or otherwise, be lent, resold, hired out or otherwise circulated, without the publisher's prior consent, in any form of binding or cover other than that in which it is published.

www.ukiyoto.com

PREFACE

Love is an absolute feeling of deep affection. It cannot be defined in a sentence or a stanza. No one knows when one will feel it. Everything looks beautiful and fascinating under love's bower. Life fills with desires and dreams and becomes more meaningful.

The desire to live with him or her forever and ever never ends. This thought itself runs from the heart to the mind through the nerves and blood. For centuries millions of poets and writers have expressed their thoughts, ideas, and views on Love and have enriched us through their literature.

In the intricate tapestry of human existence, few threads are as profound and as poignant as the one woven by love. It is a force that propels us to the highest peaks of ecstasy and plunges us into the deepest abysses of despair. Love is both the light that illuminates our path and the shadow that haunts our dreams. It is a journey fraught with joy, but also with pain.

In "Love, the Destiny to Pain," the poet embarks on a poetic odyssey through the myriad facets of love—its beauty, its betrayal, its separation, its loneliness, and its sadness. Within these pages, you will find a collection of verses that delve into the depths of the human heart, exploring the complexities of relationships, the scars left by betrayal, the ache of separation, the solitude of loneliness, and the melancholy of unrequited love.

As one journeys through the pages, he/she may find solace in the shared experience of love in all its complexity.

Thank you all.

With love,

Spondon Ganguli

Acknowledgements

First and foremost, I express my gratitude to God Almighty for granting me the strength, knowledge, ability, and opportunity to translate my thoughts into poetry. Without His blessings, this endeavour would not have been conceivable.

To my beloved wife, Smt. Somasree Ganguli, I owe an immeasurable debt of gratitude for her unwavering patience, love, and relentless encouragement throughout the process of crafting these poems. Her pride and enthusiasm in my work serve as a constant source of inspiration.

I extend my heartfelt thanks and profound respect to Mrs. Papia Ghosh (Pal), my mentor and guiding light since 2019, whose wisdom and guidance have been instrumental in shaping my journey as a writer and poet. Her support and unwavering faith in my abilities have been indispensable in bringing this book to fruition.

In remembrance and with deep appreciation, I honour the memories of two individuals whose influence on my writing journey continues to resonate profoundly. The invaluable ideas and suggestions of the Late Sri Satadal Lahiri, as well as the visionary belief in my potential as an author by the Late Sri Puspen Mukherjee, have left an indelible mark on my creative endeavours. To these departed souls, I offer my deepest respects and heartfelt tributes.

I am profoundly grateful to Ukiyoto Publishing for their invaluable support and assistance in bringing this book, "Love: The Destiny to Pain," to fruition. Without their dedication and partnership, this project would not have come to fruition.

Spondon Ganguli

Contents

Our First Date…	1
He has no choice but to kiss him	3
Echoes of Departed Love	4
You are My Breath, My Life…	6
Love's Strength Unites Us	8
Eternal Journey of Love	9
I Must Depart, My Friend	11
An Unsung Melody	13
Echoes of Friendship through Time	15
Kiss me	17
For you, I breathe	18
Belonging to You Alone	20
For You, My Beloved Angel	21
In Midnight's Veil, I Stood	22
You Are My Angel	24
Everlasting Desires	25
Remembering You Through Time	26
Still, He is Mine	28
In Search of You	29
My Missing Love	31
You and I	32
A Farewell Kiss	34
My First Letter…	36

Whispers of Togetherness	39
Unheard Echoes of the Heart	40
Echoes of Anticipation	41
She has no choice but to kiss…	43
Symphony of Love	45
Goodbye	46
My Schoolmate	48
Together Through the Storm	50
A Song Unheard	52
Echoes of New Bonds	53
Echoes of Absence	54
Harmony of Hearts	56
Echoes of Us	58
Waiting in Silence	60
Essence of Love	61
End of Love	62
Promise of Remembrance	64
Echoes of Love	65
Footsteps of Betrayal	66
Journey Beyond Farewell	67
Winter of Longing	68
A Song Unheard	70
Divine Serenade	71
My completeness	72
For me, you are the reason	73
When death arrived…	74

My Little Heart 76

About the Author 77

Our First Date…

Do you remember the first date we went on?
You held my hand and pressed my palm with care.
You thought for a while and took me on your back.
You smiled and whispered, "Let's move on, my doll."

They gave a look at us, we seemed rare.
"Even a boy kissed a girl, here matters..."
How come you became so brave? It's the effect of love.
From that, I, too, can't remain safe.

I felt as if it could be snow as morning dew.
I kept imagining if it could rain!
Let's go to the lake, do you know how to swim?
No... Don't you fear? Why? You will take me

On your back there, are we alone here on a boat?
The sunset past an hour, as the dusk appeared.
You asked, let's move if you are ready.
I asked you for a Teddy.

You said, "Boys don't play with a soft toy."
I replied, "Then 'Boys' don't love a boy."
It's difficult to convince you.
B'caz, you love me, and I love you.

Are we the sacred couple dove?
You are the one and only one I love.
And the story ends here,
Hope memories are still alive.

He has no choice but to kiss him

In a world where fate's decree is clear
He stands, entwined in destiny's scheme
Two souls collide, an echo drawing near
He has no choice but to kiss him, it would seem

Bound by threads of unseen force
Their hearts converge in a silent plea
A moment's touch, a fate-endorsed
He has no choice but to kiss him, free

Though doubts may cloud his inner sky
He feels the pull, a magnetic stream
Their souls align, no reason why
He has no choice but to kiss him, it would seem

In this union of souls, he finds his grace
Their lips meet softly, love's sacred hymn
Embracing love's dance, a warm embrace
He has no choice but to kiss him, free

Echoes of Departed Love

Amidst the chaos, a lost soul I dwelled,
Till your arrival, a story to be unveiled.
You grasped my hand, unlocking a door,
A realm of love and joy did you implore.
Yet now, your absence outweighs the love you gave,
An empty ache, a burden hard to stave.
Petals inquire, leaves whisper your name,
In gentle rustles, your presence I reclaim.
Each stolen glance finds your room's padlock,
My thoughts stray from tasks, my mind in shock.
A reunion with old friends, I avoid their gaze,
Unanswered queries in their eyes, a silent phrase.
Nightly, my bed cradles a hollow space,
My childhood relics, my room's embrace misplaced.
Longing for your arms, your scent in the air,
In the dark, a maddening void to bear.
Reasons are hidden, you departed without a word,
Silent mysteries, my thoughts often stirred.
On that day, abandoned, I wept and cried,
Loneliness and sighs intertwined, side by side.

Words that hurt, wounds buried deep,
A precipice's edge, secrets I keep.
Each day I mourn my own foolish strife,
Loneliness is the blade that takes my life.
Hope flickers still, a chance to renew,
Days pass, diverging paths, just us two.
In the midst of Life's relentless flow,
You and I tread separate roads, our destinies aglow.

You are My Breath, My Life…

You are my breath, my life's embrace,
Yet life's tapestry is more than just one face,
For oxygen alone cannot sustain,
We need connection, love's gentle rain.

When someone binds their heart to yours or mine,
There's no need for worry, no need to pine,
Love, like oxygen, fuels eternity's flame,
Immutable feelings, none can tame.

Just as night begets the brighter day,
From sadness, we seek joy's array,
My love for you grows potent and true,
Challenges only deepen the hue.

In our love, let trust forever bloom,
Mature your thoughts, dispel the gloom,
United by a celestial thread,
Fear not, for where our souls are wed.

Though anger and shouts may find their place,
Like ECG curves, life's endless chase,
Through ups and downs, our bond prevails,
A straight line's end, love never entails.

Our life thrives through empathy's song,
Love's Symphony, forever strong,
Together we'll stand, as days dance away,
Or cherish each memory, come what may.

When destiny calls, and we must part,
Remember, love's imprint on the heart,
So fear not the unknown, my dear,
For in love's embrace, we conquer every fear.

Love's Strength Unites Us

In storms, I hold no fear, you see
Beside you, strong, my knight in light
Together, brave, we face the sea
Lonely thoughts take flight, out of sight

With you, my saviour, ever near
My life's fulfilled, love's endless art
Guided by dreams, no need for fear
Hand in hand, we'll never part

Through staggered steps, our journey's grace
My fingers seek your steady clasp
In wavering times, your steadfast face
Holds firm through every trial's rasp

Your shoulder, refuge, sure and sound
Though knocked, I rise; your grip holds tight
In you, my anchor, I am found
Together, we conquer the darkest night

Eternal Journey of Love

Upon my heart's soft stage,
I long to convey,
Beloved, you're my very soul,
My partner, true love's role,
Found in the light of day.

Beside you, let me stride,
On the sands of the shore,
Footprints fleeting, yet wide,
Moments to adore, explore,
In love's gentle tide.

Together, let's take flight,
To skies above, so high,
Where lucky stars unite,
In cosmic lullaby,
Forever in love's light.

Through oceans, hand in hand,
We'll glide with grace,

Horizon's distant land,
Cupid's tender embrace,
Our love, vast as the sand.

Let me cherish and adore,
Tenderness is so true,
Journey's path we explore,
In each step, a new,
Our destiny, evermore.

I Must Depart, My Friend

I must depart, my dear friend,
Do not impede my journey's trend.
Your tearful gaze, a plea so clear,
Yet, I must venture without fear

I'm bound for distant realms, you see,
A path is uncharted; destiny beckons me.
Though your voice calls in the wind,
My steps I must courageously rescind.

Embracing arms, warmth so true,
They beg me to stay, to remain with you.
But my path is set, a road unknown,
Afraid to linger, my heart was overthrown.

A traveller through time's vast sea,
My destiny remains an enigma to me.
A nomad of existence, I must tread,
For the betterment of mankind ahead.

So let me go, release my hand,
In the tapestry of life, I must expand.
Though parting stings, a bitter fray,
Forward I march, on this destined day.

An Unsung Melody

The song within me yearns to rise,
Yet remains veiled in silent skies.
I've woven and unwoven the threads,
Of words that dwell in my heart's stead.

The moment, a whisper in the mist,
Words unformed, a tale dismissed.
Within, the ache of dreams denied,
Yearning to bloom, to reach beside.

His visage, unknown to my eyes,
His voice from a distant echo that flies.
Yet, footsteps soft on my path they tread,
A melody of anticipation's thread.

But the lamp's flame flickers low,
I dare not invite him nor let him know.
Within hope's dwelling, I bide my time,
Awaiting our meeting in the future's rhyme.

So let the unsung song persist,
In the quiet chambers, it exists.
A symphony of hearts yet apart,
We dance to the rhythm of an unsung art.

Echoes of Friendship through Time

Oh, dear friend, where now dost thou reside?
Memories of us, do they still coincide?
In the embrace of age, we both now stand,
Awaiting a reunion, hand in hand.
The schoolyard days, etched in my mind's embrace,
Shared laughter and lessons in that vibrant space.
Lost are the threads that wove our paths anew,
Yet, still, I ponder, where could you be, too?
No kisses shared embraces warm,
Through misunderstandings, we weathered life's storm.
Your reassuring touch, a steady guide,
In moments of need, you stood by my side.
They speak of lovers, stars in the night,
But your presence eludes both dream and sight.
Though absent in stars that twinkle above,
The love I hold for you is true and unwavering.
In the dance of rebirth, if fate allows,
Could we cross paths again, as time avows?

Would our bond endure, just as before?
As kindred spirits in life's grand encore.
Gender anew, yet hearts unswayed,
Would love's bloom flourish, unafraid?
Time's secrets lie hidden, yet hope shall unfurl,
In the tapestry of life, let destiny twirl.

Kiss me

The day I first met you on my bed,
I was sixteen.
My heart felt the vibe when the soul
got its wing.

You held me on your bare chest,
And I found myself in Angel's nest.

You asked, "What's up! My dear?"
"Love you" was all I wanted to say but feared.

The vision got blurred,
As the two lips touched.
I felt within you,
As if I am getting dissolved.

Then I woke up from sleep,
And found myself lost in the dream.

For you, I breathe

I screamed "GOAL!" and everybody stood like a fool.
You all jumped over me, and I went flat on the ground.

No one noticed your smile.
While passing the ball to me.
No one noticed your fingers
touching my cheeks.

I smiled back and said, "Thanks"
When you said, "I am proud of you."
I blinked my eyes and softly whispered,
"I love you."

Didn't you hear that?
You didn't notice my eyes!

You got carried away with the game
For the loss and the win.
But my heart beats for you

at every step in the field.

You get on my nerves
When it's time to say bye!
I go crazy on
Your smile and your jubilant vibe.

I know that I am gay.
But to you, how could I say?
It will be painful if you leave me alone.
It will be painful to see you go away.

Hope the day will come you will understand me.
Till then, let me be your best friend only.

Belonging to You Alone

He called me that night,
Out of fear's tight grasp!
His legs, like quivering reeds,
Eyes agape, a universe unfurled.

I gazed upon him, arms unfurled,
A haven within my tender breast.
He wore vulnerability like a child's cloak,
His eyes are mirrors of an ocean's mist.

"Stay, I beseech," he whispered, fragile plea,
Yet, fate's hand guides my steps to go,
For should we linger, love entwined,
The world's cruel gaze, unyielding blow.

But the path of devotion calls my name,
A journey to tread, though hearts may yearn.
In shadows, we'll meet; in secrets, we'll reside,
A love unbound, like stars that burn.

For You, My Beloved Angel

My beloved Angel, unto me you came,
Life's saviour, love's sentinel aflame,
Among a thousand bees, one to claim.

I know within me, a truth does stay,
A secret whispered, night and day,
In thoughts of you, my heart's display.

I'm gay, not as the world may see,
Yet, your essence is what sets me free,
A truth that's real, unshackled, and key.

So what if my heart's compass turns,
Towards paths uncharted, desires that churn,
In you alone, my passion's fire shall burn.

Not girls, not boys, a singular view,
In the spectrum of love, it's only you,
My feelings are pure, my devotion true.

In Midnight's Veil, I Stood

To the terrace, in midnight's cloak, I tread,
A wanderer in sleep's shrouded thread.
Mother's words echoed, tales of nocturnal roam,
Yet, my room's bounds were childhood's home.

A silhouette upon the terrace's rim,
Gazing at the moon's ethereal hymn.
Step by step, I drew near, my heart awhirl,
He turned, and my senses did unfurl.

Was it truly you, or dream's tender seam?
Could we bridge a gap, surreal as it may seem,
Two decades' chasm, traversed in the night,
Temporal boundaries melted, out of sight.

"Why this distance, a chasm wide?
Draw near, embrace, hearts collide."
"I yearn for a kiss," he spoke, eyes sincere,
A moment suspended, a choice to adhere.

"No, my dear, a kiss I can't partake,
For life's complex web, it's too much at stake.
A gift I bear, a letter of fate's decree,
Two initials inscribed, a mystery."

In his hand, the missive lay,
A world contained in what he'd say.
My memory falters, my consciousness fleeting,
Mother's presence and my bed, reuniting.

On the terrace's edge, or in the dream's domain,
Tears stream down, love's bittersweet rain.
Recollections surge, love's depths I dive,
Nandan, unspoken love, forever alive.

"Did you truly appear, or dream's fleeting gleam?
In the still of the night, was it truly you I'd seen?"
Unfolding the letter, penned gracefully,
"Please don't weep, goodbye, in letters three."

You Are My Angel

I set the stage for nature's play,
Let blossoms caress your lips so fey,
Fresh leaves grace your cheeks; they stay,
As joyous birds serenade the day.

Raindrops fall in rhythm's trance,
A dance of nature's sweet romance,
A breeze whispers secrets, wild and free,
Heartbeats echo in each soul's decree.

An Angel descends, eyes of azure hue,
Heaven's gift, radiant and true,
On bended knee, a gesture kind,
Cupping your visage, tenderly entwined.

At that moment, a tapestry of feelings,
Sorrow and joy, emotions reeling,
Wings enfold, embrace the divine,
A union of souls, a love's design.

Everlasting Desires

An angel, veiled in human guise,
Stepped into my world, a blessed surprise.
I witnessed his eyes transform, cerulean and deep,
Gazing at me, moments I wished to keep.
In torrents of rain, his wings unfurled,
Enveloping my essence, a shelter for the world.
A fleeting touch, a momentary hue,
Startled from slumber, emotions anew.
How could his warmth linger, ethereal and clear,
As if his presence dwelled close, ever near?
I yearn for his embrace, a haven from distress,
A refuge in tears, in fear's tender caress.
Oh, to have him by my side, my guiding light,
In moments of anguish, in the darkest night.
An angel in human guise forever wanted,
To hold me close, as dreams are haunted.

Remembering You Through Time

In a time, that's spanned more than twenty years,
Yet vivid, the day at eighteen appears.
Today, wedded, my heart finds its home,
A loving wife by my side, I've come to own.

Through day and night, her care's embrace,
In her love, I've found a cherished space.
As life's complete man, I stand tall,
With her, I've been blessed with a child, my all.

A year has passed, and a baby boy to hold,
In his innocence, my heart unfolds.
His eyes, his nose, his cheek, his chin,
Echo the face I yearned to win.

His tiny steps, his hugs so tight,
His radiant smile, his words of light,
They take me back to dreams of old,
When nineteen, your memory I'd hold.

Blessed I am, to call him my son,
A priceless treasure, second to none.
Bestowed by divine grace above,
I've named him after you, my love.

Is it wrong to feel you so near,
In the laughter of my child so dear?
As your essence in him, I find,
A thread of past and present twined.

Still, He is Mine

He spurned the love I offered true,
His inner turmoil, a mystery unscrewed,
Deep within, emotions we'd share,
Yet I remain hopeful, beyond despair.

Love's embrace, our hearts did yearn,
A flame within, forever to burn,
I won't relent, won't let him flee,
For our love's essence, a bond to decree.

Society's chains shan't bind our fate,
Our love, unshackled, will navigate,
No shame, no fear, shall interfere,
As a new year's dawn beckons, clear.

He turned away, reasons untold,
In shadows he lingers, his heart consoled,
Still, I long to be his guiding spark,
In love's abyss, where our souls embark.

In Search of You

The verses I weave find life through you,
In tales I tell, your spirit shines true,
My words find purpose in your adoration,
Oh, how I ache in your absence, a palpable sensation.

Guiding me along an uncertain trail,
You bestowed courage, never to fail,
In moments of doubt, your grasp held tight,
Oh, how I yearn for your presence's light.

Once, you ignited the flame of my start,
A lantern in the darkness, you played your part,
My thoughts charged by your empowering plea,
Oh, how I long for you that used to be.

Have I reached my destination, my quest's end?
What victories, what triumphs might I send?
Amidst the unknown, one truth I pursue,
To have you return, my constant, my true.

You, the inspiration that fuelled my pen,
The missing piece I ache for again,
Unknown achievements, they pale, it's true,
All I desire is the return of you.

My Missing Love

A missing love, my heart's lament
He was the one, my heart's intent
Gone away, a void of immense
His touch, a memory heaven-sent

I sought him 'round, a fruitless quest
Illusion's grip, my heart suppressed
Friend and love, within his chest
His kiss, a fire, once caressed

Alone I stand, no longer pined
Left behind, my tears consigned
He urged me to start anew, remind
Yet tears still gleam, love's bind

In time he'll depart, I sense it near
To ease his path, I'll persevere
A babysitter, without fear
In love's cocoon, I'll hold him dear

You and I

You and I, divergent ways we tread
In shadows cast by words unsaid
Within, a coward's heart does dread
A flame unlit, emotions thread

I longed to burn, to be consumed
Yet life persists, leaves me entombed
Alone I stand, my heart resumed
In stillness, where my fears have bloomed

When you departed, you left me cold
My tears, a river, endlessly flowed
In solitude, my heart's tale told
But Cliff's embrace, my hands withhold

Each day a canvas painted blue
For my mistakes, I pay my due
A lonely soul, a sky of rue
Yet hope resides, my spirit true

Life's journey twists, and we're led astray
You and I, on a separate array
In silent steps, we find our way
Bound by the past, yet a new dawn may sway

A Farewell Kiss

The crimson cascade, a sight to behold
Beauty in pain, an anomaly untold
Lips locked in agony, a story unfolds
Upon the bed of endings, my destiny enfold

Curled in fetal stance, a plunge into the night
Darkness consumes a path to take flight
A distant voice whispers, love's fading light
"I'd love you endlessly if not for this plight"

Is my gender a sin? Is that my decree?
Loving sincerely, unchained and free
Denied the one I adore for all to see
A girl's claim to him, the end of my glee

Worthless, they say, a societal shame
No good, no love, just an empty name
Gender surpasses love in this cruel game
Affection denied, desire doused in flame

Can't two souls connect, regardless of kind?
Bound by devotion, in heart and mind
Love without gender, can't we redefine?
Building a family, a new fate to bind.

Unanswered queries and doubts left to bear
Perhaps from beyond, some truths we'll share
The Lord of Death's kiss, the pain to repair
In that final embrace, my soul laid bare.

My First Letter…

When I penned that initial love note in secrecy,
My dearest,

Never did I envision your heart's embrace,
To cradle my fervent affection, one distant day.
In the realm of schooldays,
I stood timid, a fragile soul,
With a heart unsteady and courage unformed.

In those youthful days, you towered,
Your presence is a symphony of allure,
Generosity woven into your very being.

When I inked that first love letter, a clandestine whisper,
Beloved,

Little did I fathom your eventual step towards me,
Amid the halls of learning,
A lone figure I often was,

Shadowed in the hue of solitude.
While you bask in the warmth of camaraderie,
A constellation of friends, ever gleaming.

How could I summon the audacity,
To hand over that letter to your keeping?
It lingered, a silent witness, within my haven,
Sealed with the essence of love,
A token preserved, etching our shared history.

Yet, a faint scar remains etched,
In the chambers of my heart,
As I watched you recede, hand in hers,
A sight that painted distance in hues of pain.

Undeniably destined, you two,
Emanating an ethereal aura,
A celestial pair.

May my well-wishes grace your path,
The day you sealed your union,
With a kiss upon the wedding cake.

As I inscribed that first love letter,
Every inch of my heart and soul poured forth,
Unreservedly, unhesitatingly,
A testament to love, selflessly laid bare.

Whispers of Togetherness

Once the day arrives for your sea's embrace,
Take me along in your journey's grace,
Will you promise to include me too?

When the day comes for your song to sound,
Let me be the listener, spellbound,
Will you assure me that it's me you'll choose?

On the day you paint a picture anew,
Keep me close, by your side, as you do,
In my heart, some fragments stay,
The brushstrokes you've shared, a bond to convey.

When you hold a pen on another day,
Filling pages with verses at bay,
Let my inspiration in you remain,
For the songs you write, my thoughts to gain.

Unheard Echoes of the Heart

Everyone heard the spoken words,
But none grasped the ache concealed,
In the bustling market's clamour,
No one sensed the silence revealed.

She was my shadow once,
Or perhaps an image of me?
From my abode, she disappeared,
No one around to witness and see.

So many words were exchanged,
Love's calculations and its thorns,
Amidst the realm of my dreams,
She was there,
the one for whom my heart mourns.

Morning's light and gentle breeze,
Shattered my slumber's hold,
Beside me, she found her place,
Someone nudged me from the cold.

Echoes of Anticipation

In silence, my intended song resides,
A melody untouched within me bides.
Days pass, and still, its notes don't find the air,
I weave and unweave my instrument with care.

The destined moment lingers, yet delays,
Words yearn to dance upon the perfect phrase.
Within, a longing grips my beating heart,
A silent wish that tears my soul apart.

His visage veiled, his voice a mystery,
Yet soft footfalls hint at his trajectory.
Upon the path that leads to my abode,
His presence, like a whisper, in me flowed.

But still, the lamp of welcome does not glow,
He stands without a stranger yet to know.
With hope as constant as the morning sun,
Anticipation lingers for our union to be spun.

Reimagined is the tune that fate shall play,
A song unsung but not cast to decay.
Its verses are now rekindled, finding a voice,
A tale of longing waiting, by my choice.

She has no choice but to kiss…

In a world where choices seem confined,
A tale unfolds of hearts intertwined.
A moment arrives, no path to detour,
She stands at the crossroads of love, unsure.

Their eyes lock in a serendipitous dance,
A tender touch, a stolen glance.
Her heart flutters like a captured bird,
Her mind entwined, her thoughts unheard.

But fate's cruel hand deals its blow,
A choice relinquished; she must bestow.
For pressures unseen, she's pushed to the brink,
To kiss another against her heart's link.

Invisible chains bind her free will,
Her heart cries out, yet she must be still.
The world may whisper, and judgments sting,
Yet deep within, she knows this isn't their thing.

For love is not forced or coerced by might,
But a symphony of souls aligning just right.
In the face of pressure, she must stand tall,
To honour her truth and let her heart call.

No choice but to kiss, they may believe,
But a loveless kiss can only deceive.
In the realm of hearts, true love does grow,
In the sacred space where souls bestow.

Let not conformity dictate her art,
For love's essence lies in a willing heart.
So, she must choose to defy the decree,
To honour her soul, to set love free.

For in love's rebellion, she finds his voice,
In following her heart, she makes the right choice.
A love that's authentic, honest, and pure,
And the kisses that are not forced but forever endure.

Symphony of Love

One stands tall, a beacon of strength,
The other exudes beauty and fire's length.
Their enchanting presence, radiant and bold,
In the spotlight, their love story is told.

With tender smiles and a gaze so sweet,
They lock eyes, two hearts in rhythm beat.
Their dance, their song, and the passionate sway,
Together, they craft a love story, come what may.

A symphony of love, strong and true,
In each other's arms, they find what's due.
Two souls entwined, a love beyond compare,
Their gay love, a testament, so rare and so fair.

Goodbye

The oozing red fluid
Had never looked so beautiful before today.
Though my lips pursued in pain
As I closed my eyes and lay down on the bed.

The fetal posture left me in the middle of the darkness
Engulfing me to another world.
I could feel a soft voice echoing afar
'I could love you forever
I could if you are not, you but a girl.'

Is that my fault? I'm a boy and not a girl
Who loved him so honestly, so pure!
Is that my fault? I can't hold him back
From a girl who has every right to him
Only because of her gender?

Yes, I'm worthless, You are right.
I was up to no good,

And overall, I would be a shame to society.
Gender should come before love
Sex matters over the custody of a relationship.

Can't two friends of the same gender
Love each other to infinity?
Can't two people love each,
Loyal to each, make a family?
Who will answer my questions?
Who will clear my doubts?
Maybe someone from the other world,
Where I'm heading to.

My Schoolmate

Oh, my friend! Where are you?
Do you remember me as I do?

I am old now, and so are you.
Let us meet again as I await you.

Do you remember the days in school I spent with you?
You, too, don't know where I am, as I don't know about you.
Let me have those days in my memory behold of you.

You were the only one whom I never kissed,
You were the one who always hugged me tight.
We misunderstood a lot, but you comforted me more,
You patted me when needed and held my hand without fear.

They say we can see the lover in the sky if we are lonely.
I never see you in the stars nor my dreams,

so, what, I feel the love for you with honesty.

What if we are reborn,
Will you be my same friend?

That time could you be my lover?
If we are again of the same gender!

Together Through the Storm

I never fear the storm.
When with you by my side.
I'm ready to go through it.
When you are my knight.
I never feel lonely,
As I know, you are my saviour.

As long as you are with me
I feel fulfilled in my life.
Let's love to lead the way
To reach the goal that was a dream.
As long as you and I are together
The horizon will never be out of reach.

Even though I stagger sometimes
My eyes always look for my fingers.
Sometimes my mind wavers.
But you who hold my dream that I have.

Even though I stagger sometimes

My arms get your shoulder.
Even though I get knocked over
I know you will never leave my hand ever.

A Song Unheard

The song I came to sing
remains unsung to this day.
I have spent my days stringing
and unstringing my instrument.

The time has not come true,
the words have not been rightly set;
only there is the agony
of wishing in my heart…..

I neither saw his face,
nor listened to his voice;
only I heard his gentle footsteps
from the road before my house…..

But the lamp has not been lit
and I cannot ask him into my house;
I live with the hope of meeting him;
but the meeting is not yet.

Echoes of New Bonds

Once upon a time, when every friendship was new,
I knew that forever would be, that much was true.
Every love felt like life's fresh embrace,
In every bond, a new love did grace.

You, with the girl, as autumn drew near,
That playful lad, whose kiss made dreams appear,
In my heart, the memory of that tender kiss,
Forever etched, in a moment of bliss.

Your face, radiant like the sun's bright gleam,
In love's union, your heart did dream.
Then, amidst the vast ocean of solitary time,
You sailed alone, with dreams sublime.

Echoes of Absence

In the silence of your absence,
I find solace in simply seeing you from afar,
in the fleeting moments of dreams,
and the memories that wrap around my heart.

There's a weight in not knowing,
why you choose to drift away,
why your voice has fallen silent,
leaving echoes of unanswered questions.

But even amidst the uncertainty,
I find a quiet strength within,
to carry on,
to hold onto the moments we shared,
like fragile treasures in the sands of time.

I may not have you by my side,
but I'll never let go of the love I hold for you,
a steady beacon in the night,
a promise to remain steadfast,

to wait for your return.

I never sought to possess your heart,
only to witness the joy in your smile,
to stand beside you through the trials,
and offer solace in the storms.

So I'll keep holding onto hope,
keep tending the flame of love,
knowing that wherever you may roam,
my heart will be here, waiting,
ready to embrace you once more.

Harmony of Hearts

The friendship that time has spun
And the love within my heart begun
Both entwined, no difference in the mind

The football match, a memory bind
On the bench, in the park, we find
Meaning in moments that the heart does start

Do you still come, to that corner depart?
In my dreams, to the world we chart
Left behind, in a place where dreams are confined

I feel joyous, I feel a pang
Your presence lingers, a sweet harangue
In both my days and dreams, where emotions hang

The match you won, my heart, you've won
In the shade of trees, their leaves undone
For our love holds sway, as time sways away

The books we share, ownership astray
Reciting poems, a sweet ballet
Do you recall, the day we shed tears all

Echoes of Us

Friendship grows, a vine in time's embrace,
Love nurtured, a constant beating in my heart,
Mind's realm holds no boundary for their dance.

The football match, a memory's flicker,
On the corner bench in the park's repose,
Meaning carved in the chambers of the heart.

Do you still come, and perchance linger?
In dreams, I wander to the world we left,
A realm of echoes where our footsteps trod.

Happiness and sadness, interwoven threads,
Your presence woven into the fabric of my days,
And dreams painted with hues of your essence.

The match, a victory etched in the chronicles,
My heart, a captive of our shared love,
Trees shedding leaves as witnesses to our tale.

Books, repositories of shared narratives,
Ownership fades, the essence remains,
Reciting poems, a mutual exchange of souls.

Do you recall, in the mosaic of time,
The day when tears flowed from both our eyes?

Waiting in Silence

I don't know why you went away,
Or why you've been so silent.

Seeing you from afar is enough for me,
A hug when my heart is lonely brings happiness,
Meeting you in dreams is already great.

In this moment, I feel you might not be in my life,
But I am ready to carry on.
Remembering the time when I had you every moment brings joy.

What I know is, I'll never walk away from you,
I'll be the one waiting for your return.
No matter when or if someone hurts you,
I'll be there to help you heal.
I never wanted to own your heart,
All I want is a smile on your face.
This assures you I'm not in a race,
But the love I gave to you is my heart.

Essence of Love

How can I hate him whom I love so dear?
How can I miss him when he's in my heart?
His essence in each breath, so close, so near,
His presence felt within me, every part.

He gives me strength to weather every storm,
And fills my heart with love so pure and true.
He came to me and took a human form,
Fulfilled my thirst for the divine, anew.

He brought me dreams that grant me fearless sleep,
And merged with me to live a life of grace.
His memory in my soul, I deeply keep,
How can I hate him with his loving face?

How can I miss him when he's always here?
How can I hate him whom I hold so dear?

End of Love

I can't love you anymore,
So many questions still remain in my mind.

Every pain you gave to me,
The tears that rolled down...
The suffering you thrust on me,
The smile I bear on my face...

I seek help from my stars
To find the strength,
To gain the patience.
I dreamt of your love...

Those days and times
Will never come back...
I never forced you
To look down on me
In the crowd of hundreds.

Why is it like this?
We're searching for
The reason that...
I understand, goes wrong.

Even if the tears
That flowed down,
Have you ever
Wondered why?
It might be because
You made me happy or sad.
I don't know what,
But I just can't love anymore.

Promise of Remembrance

Distance may part us, but thoughts won't cease,
We're just an arm's length away, our hearts release.

I promise you, I'll always keep in mind,
Through good and bad, joy and pain combined.
I'll cherish every moment that we shared,
Till my final breath, your memory ensnared.

I promise you, I'll tend to nature's bowers,
Recalling days with you among the flowers.
I pledge to hold your memory close, no less,
Love enduring, beyond life's final caress.

I vow to remember, till my very last breath,
My love for you, transcending even death.

Echoes of Love

In the storm's embrace, I fear no harm,
With you, my knight, beside me strong and warm.
Loneliness fades with you as my saviour,
Together, we faced life's trials with fervour.

But now, as shadows lengthen and time slips away,
I grasp at memories, where love used to stay.
Hand in hand, we once chased our dreams,
Now distant echoes in silent streams.

Through life's uncertainties, I sway and fall,
Your absence echoes, a silent call.
In tears, I find solace, though you're gone,
Forever in my heart, where you belong.

Footsteps of Betrayal

To my heart,
I would like to say
Darling, you were my soul,
My companion and true love
I thought I discovered.

Let me walk with you,
On the sand beach,
Leaving the footsteps,
Though they were not permanent.

Let me fly with you
To the seventh sky,
Touch the lucky star
That bound us together, but not forever.

Let me swim with you
Across the ocean,
To meet the horizon
Where Cupid once played his love tunes.

Let me love you,
Care for you,
Accompany you
In every step you put
On this beautiful earth.
But now I see our path diverges,
As betrayal stains our destiny.

Journey Beyond Farewell

I have to go afar, my friend
Do not stop me here
Your tear-filled eyes
Will not let me go
I'm afraid to step ahead.

I have to go afar, my friend
Do not call my name
Your loving arms
Will halt my feet
I'm afraid to look back.

I am a traveller of time,
My destiny is nowhere,
I cannot stay forever.
For the sake of mankind,
I have to move on.

Winter of Longing

This winter, it's not snowing, but my heart.
This winter, it's not the wind blowing, but my dreams.
And you kept me waiting outside.
I'm there for you forever,
Here, the season arrived for love.

You are my love, you are my dream,
You are my hope, my ice cream,
On this beautiful day, I want you in my life.
I'm there for you forever,
Here, the season arrived for love.

In frosty nights, my heart beats slow,
A silent echo in the icy glow.
Yet in your warmth, I find my flame,
I'm there for you forever,
Here, the season arrived for love.

Through the chill, our love will thrive,
In this winter, we'll keep alive.

For in your arms, I find my home,
I'm there for you forever,
Here, the season arrived for love.

A Song Unheard

The song I came to sing
remains unsung to this day.
I have spent my days stringing
and unstringing my instrument.

The time has not come true,
the words have not been rightly set;
only there is the agony
of wishing in my heart…..

I neither saw his face,
nor listened to his voice;
only I heard his gentle footsteps
from the road before my house…..

But the lamp has not been lit
and I cannot ask him into my house;
I live with the hope of meeting him;
but the meeting is not yet.

Divine Serenade

You promised to sing for me, my divine,
Your song will bring peace, eternal and fine.
The melody of love, forever to stay,
You promised to sing for me, come what may.

May my soul be swept in Your rhythm so true,
May my heart be enchanted by tunes meant for You.
The notes and the cadence, draw me near,
To You, my Lord, whom I hold so dear.

You, the keeper of souls, the master of bliss,
You, the divine flutist, whom none can dismiss.
You promised to sing, and I wait patiently,
For Your song to bestow eternal serenity.

My completeness

When I am on the verge of leaving
Please come to me!
When I am on the bed of bliss
Please come to me!

I want to hold your name over my mind and soul
I want to hold your hand so that
My self will be out of all fear.

I wish my final bed on the stream of the Milky Way
Where You rest your lotus feet.

I want to overcome the sorrow and the joy
They become meaningless when I see your smile.

Please don't leave me alone to cry
Don't come late to see me in grief!

Don't forget my Lord to bring your beloved too
So that to see the completeness of you.

For me, you are the reason

I am a person with a million sins.
I am a person with a million lies.
But with you, my Lord!
They can't defile my soul.

I was the person
Met died a thousand deaths.
I was the person
Reborn a thousand times.
But for you, my Lord!
I don't want salvation.

You came to me in a thousand form
But I failed to see.
You incarnated here several times
But I refused to go.
I know that you are kind enough to forgive.
If I don't exist, others will never get you too.

When death arrived…

As the end came at the threshold
I feel festive all around me.
It filled my soul with all colours and joy,
To meet you, my Lord, finally.

At the verge of the end of this life,
I know the time has arrived.
I am not in fear; I am not in shame,
For your love, I have strived.

I only want the smile to kiss my lips,
And your name is with me.
With every breath, I feel your grace,
Your love is my eternal key.

In the stillness, I sense your face,
Guiding me through this final embrace.
No more burdens, no more pains,
In your light, I find my solace.

Just the gentle falling of a celestial rain,
Your light surrounds, your voice sustains.
As I cross the threshold, I find,
With you, my soul aligns.

Here, time ceases, the soul is free,
In your arms, eternity.
A journey ends, yet begins anew,
Forever and always, I am with you.

My Little Heart

My little heart wants to be free
It wants to fly up high
To touch the centre of the galaxy
And to swim in the stream of the Milky Way.

Oh, My Lord!
Your lotus feet playing with the holy water
As a child plays when his mother bathes him.

Oh, Nature Mother!
You are lucky enough,
To have him, The Lord
As your child for the time being.
God only knows,
What is present in the future –
War or peace!
War destroys, on the one hand,
But allows a new beginning.
Peace preserves whatever is created,
Whatever exists with motherly care.

About the Author

Spondon Gaguli

Spondon Ganguli, the author of several engaging books, has a creative journey that extends beyond the written word. He showcases his multifaceted talents as an educator and artist through a dynamic website. Discover more about Spondon Ganguli's captivating world at *https://spondonganguli.com/*

www.ingramcontent.com/pod-product-compliance
Lightning Source LLC
LaVergne TN
LVHW041540070526
838199LV00046B/1757